S0-BOB-111

"I DON'T LIKE CHOOSE YOUR OWN ADVENTURE® BOOKS. I *LOVE* THEM!" says Jessica Gordon, age ten. And now kids between the ages of six and nine can choose their own adventures too. Here's what kids have to say about the Skylark Choose Your Own Adventure® books.

"These are my favorite books because you can pick whatever choice you want— and the story is all about you."
—**Katy Alson,** *age 8*

"I love finding out how my story will end."
—**Joss Williams,** *age 9*

"I like all the illustrations!"
—**Savitri Brightfield,** *age 7*

"A six-year-old friend and I have lots of fun making the decisions together."
—**Peggy Marcus** *(adult)*

Bantam Skylark Books in the Choose Your Own
    Adventure® Series
Ask your bookseller for the books you have missed

RUNAWAY SPACESHIP

SUSAN SAUNDERS

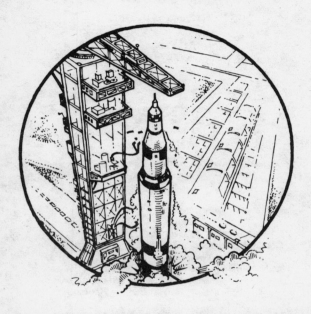

ILLUSTRATED BY TED ENIK

An Edward Packard Book

A BANTAM SKYLARK BOOK®
TORONTO · NEW YORK · LONDON · SYDNEY · AUCKLAND

RL 2, 007–009

RUNAWAY SPACESHIP
A Bantam Skylark Book / September 1985

CHOOSE YOUR OWN ADVENTURE® is a registered
trademark of Bantam Books, Inc.

Original conception of Edward Packard

Skylark Books is a registered trademark of
Bantam Books, Inc.
Registered in U.S. Patent and Trademark Office
and elsewhere.

Front cover art by Randy Jones.

ISBN 0-553-15344-7

Published simultaneously in the United States and Canada

Bantam Books are published by Bantam Books, Inc. Its trademark, consisting of the words "Bantam Books" and the por-
trayal of a rooster, is Registered in U.S. Patent and Trademark
Office and in other countries. Marca Registrada. Bantam
Books, Inc., 666 Fifth Avenue, New York, New York 10103.

PRINTED IN THE UNITED STATES OF AMERICA

CW   0 9 8 7 6 5 4 3 2 1

For Andrew Yancovitz

READ THIS FIRST!!!

Most books are about other people.

This book is about you!

What happens to you depends on what you decide to do.

Do not read this book from the first page through to the last page. Instead, start on page one and read until you come to your first choice. Then turn to the page shown and see what happens.

When you come to the end of a story, go back and start again. Every choice leads to a new adventure.

Are you ready to take a ride on a runaway spaceship? Then turn to page one—and have fun!

You are visiting your cousin Sally in Florida. **1**
Sally's father, your uncle, works as an aero-
space engineer at Cape Canaveral. He has
invited the two of you to have lunch at the
Cape. Now he's showing you around the
space center.

You and Sally walk through the building
where booster rockets are joined to space
capsules. And you climb up on a giant
crawler, which moves the spaceships out to
their launchpads.

Then your uncle gets a phone call and has
to leave for a few minutes. "Wait here; we'll
look at this next," he tells you, pointing to a
small spaceship.

Sally doesn't want to wait. She pays no
attention to the sign warning: KEEP OUT. She
ducks under some ropes and starts climbing a
ladder on the side of the small spaceship.
"Come on!" she orders.

Before you know it, you're both inside the
ship!

Turn to page 3.

All around you are switches and buttons and dials. Sally pulls the door closed. You know you shouldn't be here, but it *is* pretty exciting.

"Look," you say to Sally. "Real goldfish. And two little beds—for chimps, I bet."

Sally is poking around near a control panel. "All these loose wires," she says. "Someone could trip over them." Sally twists the wires together. . . .

Brrroooommmm! The spaceship roars to life!

"Pull those wires apart!" you shout. But the rocket fuel is already burning. You rush to the porthole. The ship is lifting off! There's a sign near the launchpad: UNMANNED MARS PROBE.

You're on your way to Mars—unless you shut off the power. But how? And if you shut it off now, you might crash.

*If you try to shut off the power,
turn to page 9.*

*If you think you had better take the ride,
turn to page 15.*

4   The two of you creep down the hall, peeking into room after empty room. Finally, you slide open a door to a huge room filled with shiny metal equipment.

"Maybe the aliens fix things here," you say. Then you pick up something silvery, about the size of your hand. "Sally!" you cry. "What does this look like?"

Sally takes a close look. "Our spaceship!"

So that's how the aliens got you on board. Somehow they shrank your ship and pulled it into theirs.

"We've got the ship," you say. "Now we'd better get out of here!"

"What are we going to do with a four-inch spaceship?!" Sally asks. "The aliens must have made *us* bigger again—with an enlarger or something. It might be right in this room. Let's look for it!"

If you look for the aliens' enlarger, turn to page 10.

If you decide to take your tiny ship and escape now, turn to page 35.

6   You're sure the room you were in is to the right. You run that way, pulling Sally along. You open a door—it's not the right room. You fling open another door—another empty room.

This must be it. You push the door open. You're standing face to face with a huge green fish!

"Greetings, aliens," the fish says, gurgling.

"You speak English!" you exclaim.

"I know many languages," the fish replies.

"Anyway, *you're* the alien," Sally says angrily. "What are you doing on *our* planet?"

"There are too many of us," the fish answers. "We are looking through the galaxies for new oceans."

Uh-oh. Earth may be taken over by talking fish!

Turn to page 37.

You want to stop this spaceship before it gets any farther away from good old Earth. You look at the control panel. There are so many buttons. Which are the right ones to push?

You put both hands down on the panel. Then you press as many buttons as you can at one time.

"Have you gone crazy?" Sally shouts.

Even if *you* haven't, the spaceship sure has. An alarm bell starts ringing, and the ship starts to spin. It spins faster and faster. You and Sally are rattling around the cabin like marbles in a jar. Is the ship going to crash? You see spots before your eyes. Then everything goes black. . . .

Turn to page 20.

10   "Okay, let's look for the enlarger," you tell Sally. "We'll take it with us. When we're safe at the Cape, we'll make the ship large again."

You search the room, but nothing looks right. Then Sally asks, "Could this be it?" She's holding up what looks like a funnel. There's a switch on the side.

"Let's see," you say.

"No, I'll do it," Sally tells you. She points the small end of the funnel at a door-sized square of metal. She presses the switch. Suddenly the metal square is the size of a postage stamp!

"Turn that thing around," you suggest.

Sally points the large end of the funnel and presses the switch: the metal square is large again.

"That's it!" you say.

Then you hear lots of strange, gurgling noises. It sounds as though they're coming from down the hall!

"The aliens!" you cry. "Let's find that escape hatch, quick!"

Turn to page 32.

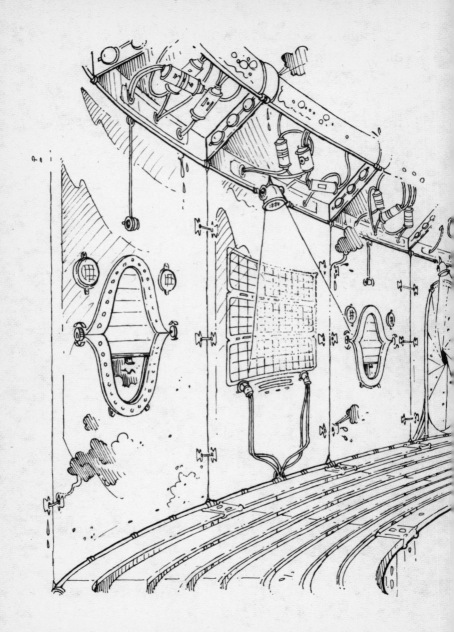

"Sally," you say, "wake up. We're on an **13** alien spaceship."

"Did our rocket crash?" Sally asks.

"If it did," you say, "I don't think we'd be here. I have a feeling *our* ship may be somewhere on *this* ship."

"What are we waiting for, then?" Sally asks, scrambling to her feet. "Let's find it!"

The two of you sneak out into the empty hallway. "We'll go this way," Sally whispers.

You follow her quietly down the long, curved hall to the left. So far, no aliens. They must all be on the other side of the doughnut-shaped ship.

Turn to page 4.

14 "Docking is too risky," you tell Sally. "We could end up as space junk." You'll let your ship do its job: fly to Mars and back.

It's not long before you wonder if you made the right choice. Three times a day the ship's computer serves your meals. Breakfast—banana flakes. Lunch—banana chips. Dinner—mashed bananas. The days stretch into weeks.

Turn to page 19.

You don't try to shut off the rocket's power **15** now. Maybe you'll do it later. Then the spaceship will be far enough from Earth to enter Earth's orbit and too far away to crash.

"Strap yourself down," you tell Sally. You lie down on one of the chimp beds and fasten the belts.

The spaceship is moving faster and faster. Minutes pass. The first booster rocket falls away, then the second. You see Sally's cap floating slowly away from her head. You're in space! And on your way to Mars, unless you think of something!

Go on to the next page.

"The people at the space center will get us down," Sally says.

"But this flight wasn't supposed to take off yet," you tell her. "How do you know their computers are even hooked up?"

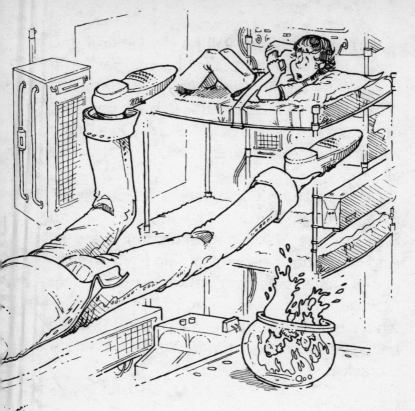

Sally isn't listening. She's floating toward the control panel. "I wonder . . ." She pushes a button.

"No!" you shout.

Turn to page 22.

18   You're sure things will go smoother if you explore on your own. You'll come back and wake Sally up later.

You peer around the door. Then you step out into the warm, damp hall. You see many rooms like the one you just left. But they are all empty.

Maybe you only imagined you saw something through that window. Maybe you and Sally are the only living things on this ship. And being alone on a robot ship from an alien planet is even creepier than seeing a live alien.

Suddenly you hear gurgling noises somewhere in front of you. You creep down the hallway toward the sounds. You open a door a crack and peek in. Aliens!

Turn to page 30.

"I like bananas," Sally says when you complain. "Besides, it only takes a year or so to get to Mars." A year! Three times 365 days—that's at least 1,095 meals of dried bananas. And there's still the trip back!

Then you spot a comet. It's a huge, glowing ball with a long tail. "I think this is the year it's supposed to fly quite close to Earth," Sally says.

If Sally's right, maybe the comet could pull your spaceship along in its tail. You could hitch a ride back to Earth!

But what if Sally's wrong?

If you hitch a ride on the comet, turn to page 27.

If you continue on to Mars, turn to page 44.

20   You finally open your eyes. Your head aches. Did you crash? You don't think so. You're lying on the floor of a large, empty room. Sally is here, too, her eyes still closed. Are you back at the space center? And where is your ship?

You look out a window—and see that you're on a spaceship shaped like a doughnut. It's moving slowly just above an ocean. Not far away are some islands.

You see someone—or some*thing*—in a window opposite you on the other side of the doughnut. Have you and Sally been picked up by space aliens?

There's a hatch in the floor. You could get out now and swim to an island. But can you be sure this is Earth?

Besides, wouldn't you like to take one good look at an alien before you leave?

---

*If you decide to get out while you can,
turn to page 24.*

*If you want to look around first,
turn to page 29.*

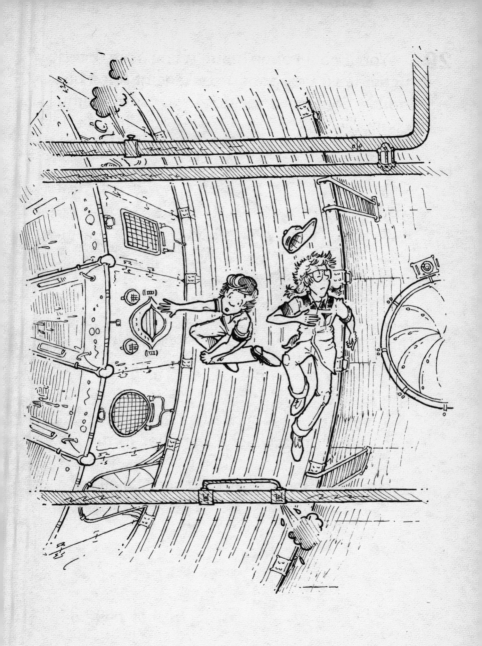

22   There's a grinding noise. A tiny door opens in the wall. Out pops a package of dried bananas. So the control panel was put in for the chimps!

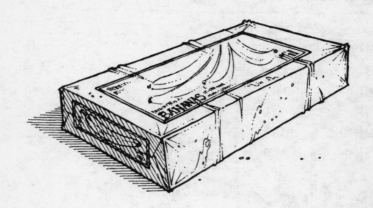

You undo your belts, float to the panel, and press a button. It fires a thruster rocket. *Whooooshh*—the spaceship dips to the right. You press another. The ship dips to the left.

So what? You're still on your way to Mars. Then Sally shouts, "An old space station!"

Turn to page 34.

You think the room with the escape hatch is to the left. You run down the hallway, dragging Sally behind you.

"They're only fish!" Sally says.

"They built this spaceship, didn't they?" you say. "Think what else they can do—to us!"

You're lucky—you find the right room quickly. You close the door and race over to the hatch. You unlock it, pull it open, and look down at the ocean below you. Just then the door to the room is flung open. It's the aliens!

Turn to page 40.

24 If this *is* an alien spaceship, it could be headed for a place a lot farther away than Mars. And you're not anxious to find out just where that might be. You unlock the hatch and pull it open. The ocean is about eight feet below you.

Now all you have to do is wake up Sally. And you'd better hurry. Whatever you saw through the window probably saw *you*, too.

"Sally! Sally!" you whisper. Her eyelids twitch. "Come on, wake up!" You shake her a little.

"What?" Sally says.

"We're getting out of here," you tell her.

"Where?" Sally asks.

"I'll explain later," you say. You pull her over to the open hatch. "Jump!"

Turn to page 42.

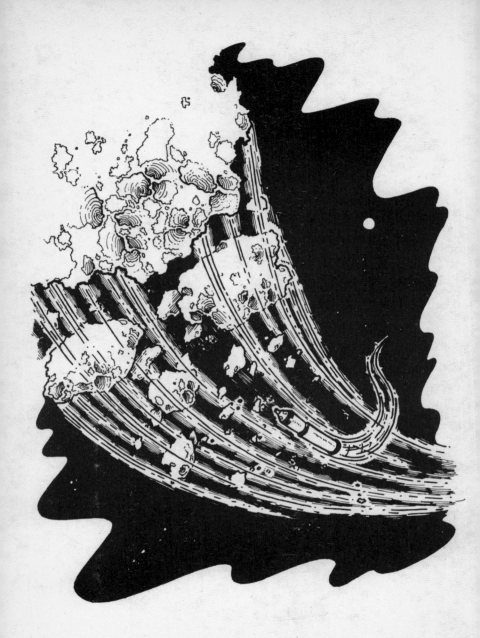

You decide to hitch a ride on the comet.
You remember reading about it in school. Besides, you're sick of bananas!

"Let's try to move the ship closer to the comet," you tell Sally. For once she doesn't argue.

You use the thrusters to push the ship forward. You're right at the edge of the comet's streaming tail. It works! The comet starts pulling the ship along, just like the pieces of rock and ice that are following it through space.

"A free ride back home!" Sally cries.

"No more bananas for us!" you shout.

There's just one problem. There are lots of comets in our solar system. One of them *will* visit Earth this year. But the others are traveling in other directions. And yours is one of the others.

It isn't long until you realize that you've traded a round trip to Mars for—a one-way trip to Pluto. You just hope the Plutonians have invented hot dogs and ice cream.

The End

If this is an alien ship, you wouldn't mind **29**
taking a closer look at an alien. And maybe
you can find out what's happened to your
own spaceship.

There's a tall, thin door in the wall opposite
the window. You tiptoe over to it. Slowly you
swing it open into an empty hallway. The air is
as hot and damp as a steambath. The aliens'
home planet must be a swamp!

You pull the door closed again. Sally is mut-
tering in her sleep, probably bossing some-
body around. Should you wake her up and
take her with you? You might find a safer way
out of here while you're exploring.

Or would it be better to leave Sally asleep
for now? She does have a way of goofing
things up. Isn't she the reason you got into this
mess in the first place?

*If you wake up Sally and take her with
you, turn to page 13.*

*If you decide to explore the ship on your
own, turn to page 18.*

30   They're aliens, all right—aliens in an indoor swimming pool! And they look like—gigantic fish! One has round scales and a tall dorsal fin like a swordfish. Another is smooth skinned and gray, with whiskers like a catfish. Still another . . .

"What's the big idea of leaving me behind?" a voice says. It's Sally, and she gives you a shove to let you know she isn't happy. Unfortunately, she shoves you right into the room

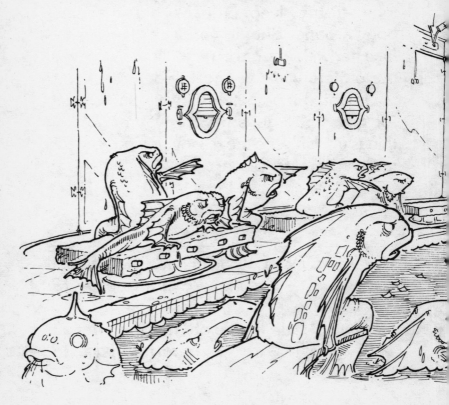

with the pool! The fishy aliens are staring at
you. And they don't look happy, either.

You grab Sally's arm and pull her back into the hallway. But now you're turned around. Is the room with the escape hatch to the right? Or is it to the left?

If you run to the right, turn to page 6.

If you run to the left, turn to page 23.

32 "It sounds like someone blowing bubbles," Sally says as the two of you dash down the hall. You sneak a peek over your shoulder. The aliens are right behind you! They look like—giant fish!

"I'll take care of them!" Sally says. She aims the small end of the enlarger at the aliens.

It's too bad you're in the way. The aliens get a lot smaller. But so do you!

"Oops!" Sally says.

Turn to page 53.

34 You float over to a porthole. Maybe you could land the ship at the space station, send a message back to Earth, and be rescued!

But the station looks so old! There may not even be air to breathe there. And you could wreck your spaceship trying to land. You're pretty sure your ship must be programmed to take you to Mars *and* bring you back safely. Maybe you ought to leave things alone.

If you decide to try to dock with the station, turn to page 38.

If you think it would be too dangerous to try, turn to page 14.

"We've got the spaceship. Now *I'm* getting out of here!" you tell Sally. "A tiny spaceship is better than none at all."

"Oh, all right," she grumbles.

You both sneak down the hall, watching for aliens. But the hallway is a dead end. There's a wall right in front of you. Then you hear gurgling sounds, very loud and very close.

"What a weird wall," Sally says. "It's all rough and scaly. Maybe there's a secret door here somewhere." She starts poking the wall.

Turn to page 46.

"Just how did we get on this ship?" Sally demands.

"Our sensors picked up distress signals from others of our kind on your rocket," the fish says. "When we rescued them, we got you, too."

What could the fish mean? Then, in silent answer, it points to a glass bowl. "They were being held prisoner," the fish says sternly.

It's the goldfish from your spaceship!

"They weren't prisoners," you explain. "They don't mind being in a bowl—they're pets."

"Then perhaps *you* won't mind," the fish says.

"Mind what?" says Sally.

"Mind being my pets on the planet Nebulon," the fish says, gurgling as guards carry you and Sally away.

The End

38   You'll try to dock with the station. Then you can radio Earth, and the space center can send up a shuttle for you.

You and Sally use the buttons on the control panel to fire the thrusters. Little by little, your spaceship moves closer to the space station. It's a huge tube, with a docking bay at one end. Four solar wings catch the sunlight. It looks like a big dragonfly. Now, if you can just line up your ship with the docking bay . . .

You miss the station completely the first time. It's harder than you thought. The second time is worse. You smash into one of the solar wings! You try to move your spaceship by firing more thrusters. But you can't pull it away. You're stuck!

Turn to page 48.

"Jump!" You and Sally hit the water at the same time. And it's not far to an island. You'll soon be safe!

But wait a minute. What did Sally say? "They're only fish." And what do fish do best of all? Swim. And that's what you'd better do right now—as though your life depended on it. Because it might—*here they come!*

The End

42   "Why should I jump?" Sally says, looking cross.

You don't have time to argue. You give her a push. *Splaattt!* Sally does a belly flop.

You're right behind her. The water is shallow and warm. And you don't have far to swim to the nearest island. Most important, you're sure this is Earth—unless they have McDonald's in outer space!

You look up. The alien ship is silently moving away. It's almost the exact color of the sky. If you didn't know it was there, you wouldn't see it at all.

Sally doesn't see it—she's splashing around very angrily. You decide to explain everything to her immediately. Then, after you reach the island, you can both decide what to tell Sally's father. You have to explain what happened to an unmanned rocket to Mars worth seventy million dollars. And your story had better be good!

The End

44   "All comets look pretty much alike," you tell Sally. "How can we be sure this is the one passing close to Earth? Let's go on to Mars."

And that's what you do. You and Sally are the first human beings to see Mars and its moons, Phobos and Deimos, close up. Your spaceship's computer sets you down on the red planet.

You put on the chimps' spacesuits and walk around on Mars. You take samples of rocks and sand to show to the people at the space center. There's nothing else around. There may be other living things in space, but not on Mars.

Now you're eager to get back to the spaceship. You certainly don't want it to start its trip back to Earth without you.

Turn to page 50.

Suddenly the wall swings around and there *is* an opening! Only it's not a door. It's edged with rows of sharp white teeth! The "wall" is a huge fish, and it's laughing!

"Guess who found the enlarger?" Sally yells.

"Just keep tickling it!" you shout. "At least if it's laughing, it can't swallow us!"

Something tells you that that gurgling noise **47**
you heard before was its stomach growl-
ing. . . .

The End

"It's time for a space walk," you tell Sally.

Luckily you've seen lots of them on TV. You find two chimp spacesuits. It's not easy putting them on. The legs are too short and the arms are too long. But finally you're dressed. You open the hatch to outer space.

Slowly the two of you work your way down the solar wing—to the tube—to the air lock. Together you turn the handle and push it open. You're inside!

Sally opens a second door into the cabin. The good news is that the air in the station is fine! The bad news is that the space station belongs to China. The astronauts are—pandas!

"What's wrong with pandas?" Sally says. "They're so cute!"

"Pandas eat only one thing," you groan. "We've just traded bananas for bamboo shoots!"

The End

50 You and Sally have just enough time to take off the chimp suits before the rocket blasts off. The ship is taking you home!

The trip back seems to last forever—too many bananas and *much* too much Sally. But you finally touch down right where it all began, at the Cape.

Everyone is so excited about your walk on **51** Mars that neither of you gets into trouble. Your pictures are in all the newspapers. You're interviewed on television. You ride in lots of parades. You even get to meet the president. And best of all, you get to stop eating bananas.

Turn to page 54.

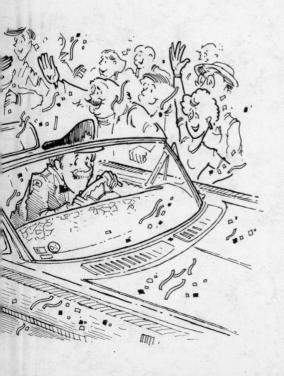

Sally scoops you up and puts you in her **53**
shirt pocket.

"Go left!" you yell in a tiny voice.

Sally doesn't hear you, but she does find
the room you were in before. She pulls open
the hatch. What if you fall out of her pocket
when she jumps? You grab hold of a button
and hang on.

Splash! Sally hits the water and starts swimming. You can't breathe! Luckily, you can just
reach a strand of Sally's wet hair. You pull
yourself up until you're out of the water. You
both reach the island safely.

"Okay," you say. "Back to my real size
now."

Sally looks kind of funny. "I dropped the
enlarger when I jumped into the ocean," she
says. "Besides," she goes on, "now you're
just the right size to fit into the spaceship."

And much too small to punch her in the
nose!

The End

54   "We're heroes all over the world," Sally says. "You have *me* to thank for all of this."

"I sure do," you say sweetly. "When are you coming to visit *us*?"

Your mom is an oceanographer. If you work it right, maybe you can strand Sally in an undersea lab for a while—with nothing to eat but fish food!

The End

ABOUT THE AUTHOR

Susan Saunders grew up on a ranch in Texas, where she learned rodeo riding. A graduate of Barnard College, she has been a ceramicist and an editor of filmstrips for children. She is the author of *Wales' Tale,* a Junior Literary Guild selection; *A Sniff in Time; Fish Fry; Charles Rat's Picnic,* also a Junior Literary Guild selection; and *The Green Slime, The Tower of London* and *Ice Cave* in the Bantam Skylark Choose Your Own Adventure series. Ms. Saunders currently lives in New York City.

ABOUT THE ILLUSTRATOR

Ted Enik is a playwright, set designer, magazine artist, and cartoonist as well as a children's book illustrator. He is the illustrator of the Sherluck Bones Mystery-Detective books, which were written by Jim and Mary Razzi and published by Bantam Books. He has illustrated a number of books in the Bantam Skylark Choose Your Own Adventure series, including *The Mummy's Tomb, The Creature From Miller's Pond* and *Summer Camp.* Mr. Enik lives in New York City.

THERE'S MAGIC IN THE AIR...

—— for winners of the ——

BANTAM/DISNEYLAND

Imagine ... you can win the ultimate dream come true ... a trip to Disneyland!

If you win our magical first prize, you, a parent or guardian and two other members of your family will be flown by U.S. Air to your luxurious accommodations at the Anaheim Hilton Hotel, right around the corner from DISNEYLAND!!

In addition, 100 runner-up prizes, a Disneyland 30th Anniversary Prize Package, will be awarded just for entering the contest.

All prizes will be chosen by a random drawing.

So don't delay, send in your entry today.

To obtain your entry coupon, and contest rules just check with your local bookseller or wherever Bantam/Begin-to-Learn™ and Bantam/Walt Disney Choose Your Own Adventure® books are sold.

No purchase necessary.

©1985 Walt Disney Productions

THE ANAHEIM HILTON
AND *Towers*

AVSK6—9/85